Acknowledgments
Designed by Liz Antill. Photographs by Tim Clark and art direction by Roy Smith. Models made by Stan and Vera Veasey of Technique and backgrounds illustrated by John Berry.

British Library Cataloguing in Publication Data

Hately, David
   Beatrix Potter's The tale of Peter Rabbit.
   —(Beatrix Potter series no. 876).
   I. Title   II. Potter, Beatrix. Tale of Peter Rabbit
   823'.914[J]   PZ7
   ISBN 0-7214-1018-9

First edition

Published by Ladybird Books Ltd Loughborough Leicestershire UK
Ladybird Books Inc Lewiston Maine 04240 USA

Text and illustrations copyright © Frederick Warne & Co., MCMLXXXVII
Based on *The Tale of Peter Rabbit* by Beatrix Potter
copyright © Frederick Warne & Co., MCMII
© In presentation LADYBIRD BOOKS LTD MCMLXXXVII

Printed in England

The tale of
Peter Rabbit

Based on the original and authorised story
by **Beatrix Potter**

adapted by David Hately

Ladybird Books
in association with Frederick Warne

Once upon a time there were four little rabbits. Their names were Flopsy, Mopsy, Cotton-tail and Peter. They lived in a burrow under the root of a big tree.

One day they were allowed to play outside. "Stay near home," said their mother. "Please don't go to Mr McGregor's garden."

"Why not?" asked Peter.

"Because he doesn't like rabbits," answered Mrs Rabbit. "He will try to catch you."

Mrs Rabbit made sure that Flopsy, Mopsy, Cotton-tail and Peter were wearing their warm clothes.

She waved them goodbye as they went out to play. Then she put on her bonnet and shawl and set off to the baker's. She wanted to buy a loaf of bread and some buns.

Now Flopsy, Mopsy and Cotton-tail were good little rabbits. They went down the lane to pick blackberries. But Peter was naughty. He ran straightaway to Mr McGregor's garden.

There were lots of vegetables in Mr McGregor's garden. Peter Rabbit loved vegetables. He began to eat them. First he tried the lettuces. Next he tried the beans. Then he ate some radishes.

Peter ate too much, because he was greedy. He began to feel sick. "I must find some parsley to nibble," he said to himself. "That will make me feel better."

Peter explored the garden, looking for the parsley. Suddenly Mr McGregor saw him and shouted, "Stop, thief!" He looked very angry, and Peter Rabbit was frightened. He ran away, but Mr McGregor ran after him.

Peter lost one of his shoes as he ran through the cabbage patch. He lost the other shoe as he jumped over the rows of potatoes. Then he started to run on four legs instead of two, and went much faster.

But Peter had forgotten the way back to the gate. He was so frightened that he didn't look where he was going. He got caught in a big net that was hanging on a gooseberry bush. Mr McGregor had put it there to stop the birds from eating his fruit.

The big brass buttons on Peter's blue jacket were tangled in the gooseberry net. He was trapped! When he saw Mr McGregor running towards him, he began to sob.

Some sparrows heard Peter sobbing, and they hopped over to see what was the matter. "Keep trying!" they chirped. "Don't give in!"

So Peter Rabbit stopped crying, and tried to free himself. And just as Mr McGregor picked up a sieve to pop over Peter's head, the little rabbit gave a tug and a wriggle and broke free! Away he ran towards a shed. But he had to leave his little blue jacket behind in the gooseberry net.

When he got inside the shed,
Peter hid in a watering can.
Mr McGregor couldn't find him
anywhere! But the watering can had
water in it, and suddenly Peter felt a
sneeze coming on. *Ker-tyschoo!* went
the sneeze. *Ker-tyschoooo!*

Mr McGregor rushed towards the watering can but Peter jumped out before Mr McGregor could catch him. He saw a little window standing open, and leaped through it. As he jumped out, he sent some potted plants flying!

The window was too small for
Mr McGregor to climb through,
so Peter had plenty of time to hide.
He saw a wheelbarrow, and crouched
behind it. When Mr McGregor came
out of the shed, Peter Rabbit was
nowhere to be seen.

Mr McGregor was very cross, and went back to his gardening.

When Mr McGregor had gone, Peter climbed up onto the wheelbarrow and looked around. He saw Mr McGregor hoeing onions. And beyond him was the gate!

Peter waited until Mr McGregor's
back was turned. Then he crept
round the paths towards the garden
gate. He squeezed under
the gate and reached
the safety of the
wood outside.
"Well done!"
chirped the
sparrows.

Back in the garden Mr McGregor hung up the blue jacket and the little pair of shoes as a scarecrow.

Peter ran all the way home. When he got there he was so tired that he flopped down on the sandy floor and closed his eyes. He still felt sick after all the vegetables he had eaten. And running away from Mr McGregor had made him feel even worse.

Mrs Rabbit was busy cooking. She noticed that Peter's jacket and shoes were missing, and she wasn't at all pleased. It was the second pair of shoes that Peter had lost in a fortnight, and the blue jacket was nearly new.

Then Mrs Rabbit took a closer look at Peter. "Dear me!" she said to herself. "His whiskers are drooping! He doesn't look very well!"

So Mrs Rabbit decided to
give Peter something
to make him feel better.
She got out her
camomile tea
and waited for
the water to boil.

Peter Rabbit groaned when he saw the tea. He knew that it tasted horrible.

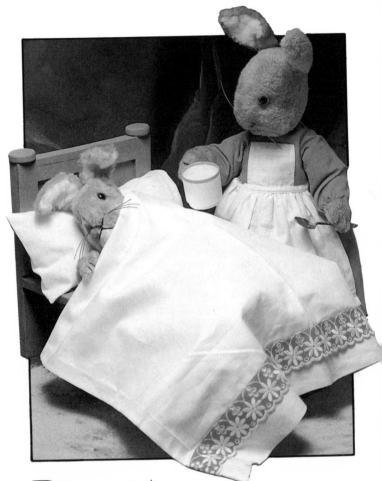

Peter was put
straight to bed and Mrs Rabbit gave
him some tea. "One tablespoonful to
be taken at bedtime," she said, as she
tucked him up.

But Flopsy, Mopsy and Cotton-tail had fresh bread, milk and blackberries for supper.

They had Peter's share, too, and they enjoyed every single bit of it.